CONTENTS

FORCED TO FLEE

Imagine being woken abruptly one morning and told you are leaving your home, all your belongings, your pets, your friends and even some of your family. You never know when or if you will see them again.

Every minute, around 25 people are forced to flee their homeland to escape war, violence or other threats. These refugees do not choose to leave. They run away to escape danger and find a safer life.

CIVIL RIGHTS STORIES

Refugees and Homelands

Written by Louise Spilsbury with illustrations by Toby Newsome

Foreword by Nelufar Hedayat

Being a refugee means accepting that the unknown place and future that you are heading to – which can be scary – is still better than staying in your homeland, which may no longer be safe. It's often very hard to explain this to people who haven't faced this situation, as me and my family did when I was a child. How much I wish I'd had this book to share with my friends, my teachers and anyone who wasn't sure how to treat me as a young refugee fleeing war in my homeland, Afghanistan.

As for young people who are in new places as refugees, I wish every one of them could read this and see themselves in this book. To see your story as a refugee told in such a caring way is precious. It gives a voice and shows that each and every one of our stories is worth telling and hearing.

Nelufar Hedayat
Refugee and journalist

Nelufar is a multi-award winning journalist and presenter who has worked across American and British Television. Her work takes her around the world, often focusing on cultural upheaval experienced by people from all walks of life, but with particular focus on women, children and families in conflict and hostile places. Nelufar has worked for a plethora of major broadcasters, from the flagship CBBC show *Newsround* to chronicling the global refugee crisis and health workers risking their lives to vaccinate children in hostile regions for Channel 4.

Rights are basic freedoms and protections everyone should have, no matter who they are or where they live.

In 1948 the United Nations (UN) – a group of 193 countries set up to help solve world problems – made a list of 30 rights for all the world's people. This important list includes the right for refugees to ask for and to be given refuge in other countries free from persecution.

EARLY REFUGEES

Throughout history, millions of people have been denied freedoms and protection. They have been forced to leave their homes to escape war or persecution.

Some 3,000 years ago, in ancient Greece, the people of Athens prided themselves on taking in people escaping from wars. Athenians believed that it was their duty to help and protect people who were persecuted and driven from their homes. They even risked their own lives to do so.

In 1685, a group of people called the Huguenots fled from France after the king threatened to punish them for following their religion. Vast numbers of Huguenots crossed to England by ship to find a safe place to worship. They settled, worked hard, set up businesses and had families.

Today, it is thought that one in six people in the UK have Huguenot ancestors.

FROM HOMELANDS TO NO LANDS

Many refugees who flee their homeland do not have official papers, such as a passport or an ID (identification) card. This means they may not be able to travel to other countries, see a doctor or get a place to live.

Without ID, refugees find it hard to get an education, work legally, start a business or open a bank account. Without a way to earn money, refugees cannot provide food, a home and medicines for their families.

Millions of people became refugees during the First World War (1914–18). Fridtjof Nansen, a Norwegian scientist and humanitarian, worked to help them. He realised that having an international identity document could help refugees make new lives for themselves.

In 1921 he created the so-called 'Nansen passport'. By 1938, this document had helped hundreds of thousands of refugees travel, and find work and new homes.

SECOND WORLD WAR REFUGEES

The Second World War (1939–45) forced 60 million people from their homes. These refugees included Jewish people who had escaped Nazi terrors. Others were people from countries invaded by the Nazis who had been taken to Germany to work, soldiers released from prison camps, and many more.

Around the world people tried to help the refugees. In a 1938–39 mission called the *Kindertransport* ('children's transport' in German), 10,000 Jewish children were brought from parts of Europe controlled by the Nazis to safety in the UK. The children had to leave their family behind and some never saw their parents again.

American social worker Martha Sharp had always worked to help people. During the war, she risked her life to rescue a group of refugee children from Nazi-occupied Europe. She brought them back to her US homeland all by herself.

This inspired other Americans to do the same. By 1945 hundreds more children were brought to safety in the US.

REFUGEE RIGHTS

The refugee crisis caused by the Second World War was so huge and desperate that new laws were written and organisations were set up quickly to help refugees.

The UN set up the International Refugee Organization (IRO) to help refugees in 1946. Within five years it had found homes for around 10 million of the 15 million refugees who were still stranded away from home. In 1952, the work of the IRO was taken over by the United Nations High Commissioner for Refugees (UNHCR).

In 1951, the UN took another important step. It came up with a special set of rights for refugees. One of the most important of these is that refugees should not be sent back to the country they came from if this puts their freedom or their life at risk.

Other rights are that refugees should have the right to work, an education and healthcare. The UN works with countries to make sure that these refugee rights are respected and protected.

HELPING REFUGEES

Hundreds of big and small groups of people help refugees in different ways. They help refugees find safe and legal routes to new homes. They may provide refugees with protection and somewhere to sleep, as well as water, parcels of food, small amounts of money, clothes, toiletries and blankets.

The way people help refugees matters. Barbara Harrell-Bond was born in 1932 in a small town in the USA, but later she travelled the world fighting for refugee rights. She changed the way people think about helping refugees.

Harrell-Bond believed that refugees had the right to take control of their own lives. For example, refugees could say what kind of food they needed and share out deliveries of food between themselves. She showed that if refugees were given the same rights and chances as others, they could start a new life and take care of themselves.

REFUGEES ON THE MOVE

Many refugees brave long and desperate journeys to get to safety. They often pay high fees to untrustworthy people to help them get away from dangerous situations. Travelling conditions are so bad that some people don't survive the journey.

More than 11 million Syrians – almost half the country's entire population – have fled their homes to escape bombs and violence since civil war started there in 2011. Many have no other choice than to travel on overcrowded boats at great risk of sinking in rough, cold seas.

In 2015, teenage Syrian swimmer Yusra Mardini was on a refugee boat that started to sink. Yusra, her older sister Sara and two others bravely leapt into the water. For three-and-a-half hours they helped to guide the boat to safety in Greece, saving the lives of those on board.

Now, Yusra works with the UN to speak up for refugees around the world.

SPORTING REFUGEES

Playing sport is about more than having fun. In sport, everyone is equal and when people play together it doesn't matter where they came from. The problem is that without a home, flag or national anthem, it's hard for refugee athletes to take part in competitions.

This all changed in 2016. During the opening ceremony of the Summer Olympic Games in Brazil, a small group of athletes marched together under the Olympic flag to the sound of the Olympic anthem. This was the first ever refugee team to compete at the Olympics.

Yiech Pur Biel raced in a running event. He fled civil war in Sudan in 2005 all alone when he was just ten years old. Pur said that he hoped by competing:

"I can show to my fellow refugees that they have a chance and a hope in life. Through education but also in running, you can change the world."
(Yiech Pur Biel, UNHCR, 2016)

REFUGEES IN CAMPS

When refugees reach a new country, they may struggle to find a place to stay. Many end up in refugee camps. These are places where thousands of people live.

Charities build camps quickly to help refugees in an emergency. As well as a place to live and sleep, refugees can get things they need, such as food and medical treatment, in the camps. Unfortunately, many camps are also overcrowded and can be damp, cold, dirty and uncomfortable.

Some refugees stay in camps for months, but others have to stay for years. Many refugees use their skills or develop new skills to help each other. As well as chefs and dressmakers, there are people such as Syrian refugee Asem Hasna, who learned to use 3D-printing technologies to make artificial limbs. His first project was a hand for a woman who had lost hers in Syria's civil war.

REFUGEE CHILDREN

Every child has the right to an education, but over half of the world's refugee children don't go to school. This may be because there are no schools nearby, they cannot afford transport to get to one, they have lost their parents and have to work, or because they cannot speak the local language.

Refugee children need an education so they can get jobs in the future, and so they can speak up for themselves and claim their rights. Learning and playing can also help children forget the bad things they have seen or experienced for a while, too.

Since 2017, a million Rohingya Muslims have fled from Myanmar to Bangladesh to escape murder and persecution. At Kutupalong, one of the biggest refugee camps in the world, Rohingya refugee teachers give children lessons and hope. They set up their own centres to teach English, maths and science to as many refugee children as they can.

CHALLENGING PREJUDICE

Some refugees face another challenge when they arrive in a new place. People there may not treat refugees fairly. People may be cruel and unkind because they think refugees are different from them. This is called prejudice.

One way to challenge and change prejudice like this is through refugee stories. Hearing about refugees' lives shows people that, while refugees may speak a different language or wear different clothes, they are ordinary people who are just trying to get the best out of life, like everyone else.

Fadak Alfayadh fled war-torn Iraq as a child. Today, she lives in Australia and travels around the country sharing her story. She tells people why she fled her home and what it's like to jump at the sound of thunder because it reminds her of exploding bombs. Her stories show people that we are all much more alike than we are different.

REFUGEE RIGHTS TODAY

The number of people fleeing their homelands has been growing in recent years. There has been a big rise in the number of refugees in Latin America.

Since 2014, over 4.5 million Venezuelans now live outside their country and the number is still rising. They are escaping starvation and danger because of a corrupt government and violent crime.

Many Venezuelan refugees flee to neighbouring countries that struggle to feed and shelter the large number of new arrivals.

In 2016, the UN made a new declaration to help the growing number of refugees around the world. It agreed that all countries should share the responsibility of helping refugees equally and fairly. That means that other countries should give money, medicines or other kinds of help to any country that welcomes refugees.

REFUGEES OF THE WORLD

Around the world people have worked hard to improve the rights of refugee people. Their efforts have made a huge difference. Many refugees have made new lives in new homelands, safe from harm. However, today there are more refugees than ever before. There are nearly 30 million refugees around the world and over half of them are children.

World Refugee Day on 20 June celebrates the courage and strength of refugees. Famous landmarks, such as the Eiffel Tower in Paris and the Empire State Building in New York, are covered in blue lights – the colour of the United Nations. People join the event to show they support refugees and to remind the world of our shared responsibility to help them.

We can all get involved by welcoming refugees who join our communities and by learning more, talking about and standing up for the rights of refugees everywhere.

REFUGEE TIMELINE

Here is a list of moments in history covered in this book that help to tell the story of the fight for refugee rights.

c. 1200–323 BCE: The ancient Greeks of Athens take in people fleeing wars and persecution.

c. 1685: The Huguenots flee France where they are persecuted for following their religion. The word refugee comes from the French word *réfugié*, which means 'gone in search of refuge'.

1914–18: The First World War causes millions of people to become refugees, fleeing from countries such as Belgium and France.

1921: Norwegian Fridtjof Nansen creates the Nansen passport – an identity document that then becomes a lifeline for many refugees.

1938–1939: The *Kindertransport* mission brings children from Germany to the UK, just before the Second World War breaks out.

1939–45: The Second World War and the violence of the Nazis force 60 million people to flee their homelands. Many are Jews who are targeted by the Nazis.

1939–45: Martha Sharp and her husband Waitstill Sharp bring refugee children, affected by the Second World War, from Europe to safety in the US.

1945: The United Nations (UN) is created. It includes the IRO – the UN organisation that is dedicated to helping refugees, and which was founded in 1946.

1948: The UN creates a list of human rights that includes the right for refugees to be allowed to move to safe countries and to receive help there.

1951: The UN decides on a special set of rights for refugees, such as the rights to work and to an education.

1967–96: Barbara Harrell-Bond works to empower refugees around the world.

2011–: Civil war in Syria forces millions to flee. Many make long and dangerous journeys to safety.

2014–: Millions begin to flee Venezuela in South America due to violence and corruption.

2015: Syrian refugees Yusra and Sara Mardini save the lives of other refugees in their boat as they cross the Mediterranean Sea to Europe.

2016: The Summer Olympic Games in Brazil is the first to have a refugee team, which included Yusra Mardini and Yiech Pur Biel. You can read about Yiech Pur Biel's role as a Goodwill Ambassador for UNHCR at: **www.unhcr.org/uk/yiech-pur-biel.html**

2017: The Myanmar government orders the army to violently force a million Rohingya Muslims into Bangladesh. The Myanmar government refuses to see the Rohingya as Myanmar citizens.

2018–: Thousands of refugees flee Central American countries, such as Honduras, Guatemala and El Salvador, due to violence, persecution, political turmoil and corruption.

GLOSSARY

abruptly suddenly and unexpectedly

ancestor a relative that you are descended from, such as a great-grandparent

ancient Greece an ancient civilisation that existed around 3,000 years ago; its lands were what is now the Greek mainland and islands

artificial human-made rather than occurring in nature

civil war a war between people who live in the same country

corrupt when an organisation or person is dishonest in return for money or power

homeland a person's home country; the country a person was born in

Huguenots French Protestants from the 16th and 17th centuries; Protestants are Christians, but not Roman Catholic Christians

humanitarian someone who works to promote better welfare or well-being for people

Jewish a person who follows the religion of Judaism

Latin America Central and South America

legal allowed by law

mission an important job, often done abroad

Muslim a person who follows the religion of Islam

Nazi a member of the National Socialist German Workers' Party; they wanted Germany to be free of Jews, homosexuals, people of colour and others

occupied a place or country taken over by the military forces of another

passport an official identity document that allows people to travel to and from different countries

prejudice when someone dislikes anyone from a particular group of people, without even knowing them

persecution to be treated badly because of your race, religion or political or other beliefs

Rohingya an ethnic group of Muslim people who live in Myanmar

social worker a person who works in the community with people suffering poverty or other hardships

United Nations (UN) an international organisation that promotes international peace, security and cooperation

The UNHCR website can be found at **www.unhcr.org**

BOOKS TO READ

Children in Our World: Global Conflict by Ceri Roberts and illustrated by Hanane Kai (Wayland, 2018)

Children in Our World: Refugees and Migrants by Ceri Roberts and illustrated by Hanane Kai (Wayland, 2018)

Forced To Flee: Refugee children drawing on their experiences by UNHCR and illustrated by refugee children from around the world (Franklin Watts, 2019)

Seeking Refuge: (series) by Andy Glynne (various illustrators), (Wayland, 2016)

INDEX

Franklin Watts
Published in Great Britain in 2022 by Hodder & Stoughton
Copyright © Hodder & Stoughton, 2022

All rights reserved.

HB ISBN: 978 1 4451 7141 8
PB ISBN: 978 1 4451 7142 5

Printed and bound in Dubai

Editor: Amy Pimperton
Designer: Peter Scoulding
Cover design: Peter Scoulding
Illustrations: Toby Newsome

Page 2 photograph
© Nelufar Hedayat

FSC
www.fsc.org
MIX
Paper from
responsible sources
FSC® C104740

Franklin Watts, an imprint of
Hachette Children's Group
Part of Hodder & Stoughton
Carmelite House
50 Victoria Embankment
London EC4Y 0DZ

An Hachette UK Company
www.hachettechildrens.co.uk

All facts and statistics were correct
at the time of printing.